Lucy the Lo

"You're coming home with us, Lucy,"
said Charlie happily, scratching the
top of the kitten's head.

"But I can't leave Rosie behind!"
Lucy mewed.

"I want to come too!" Rosie yowled.

But no one was taking any notice.

Titles in Jenny Dale's KITTEN TALES™ series

Titles in Jenny Dale's PUPPY TALES™ series

All of Jenny Dale's KITTEN TALES books can
be ordered at your local bookshop or are
available by post from Book Service by Post
(tel: 01624 675137)

Lucy the Lonely Kitten

by Jenny Dale

Illustrated by Susan Hellard

A Working Partners Book

MACMILLAN CHILDREN'S BOOKS

Special thanks to Narinder Dhami

First published 2000 by Macmillan Children's Books
a division of Macmillan Publishers Limited
25 Eccleston Place, London SW1W 9NF
Basingstoke and Oxford
www.macmillan.com

Associated companies throughout the world

Created by Working Partners Limited
London W6 0QT

ISBN 0 330 37457 5

3 5 7 9 8 6 4

A CIP catalogue record for this book is available from
the British Library.

Typeset by SX Composing DTP, Rayleigh, Essex
Printed and bound in Great Britain by Mackays of Chatham plc, Kent

Chapter One

"Look out, Rosie!" Lucy miaowed. "Here I come!" The little black kitten leaped off the ledge at the side of the pen, almost landing right on top of her sister.

"You did that on purpose!" Rosie miaowed back. She was

black too, but had a white splodge under her chin and two white paws. "I'm going to get you for that!" She playfully bashed Lucy's ear with her paw, then pounced on her sister's swishing tail.

Lucy and Rosie rolled around, locked together in one furry ball, nipping playfully at each other. They had lived at the animal shelter all their lives, sharing their big pen with three older cats – Ginger, Tammy and Winston. The other cats were snoozing in the sun at the moment, and taking absolutely no notice of the kittens. But Lucy and Rosie were used to that. They tumbled happily around the pen, stopping

only when they heard voices coming towards them.

"Have a good look round, and if you see a kitten you like, let me know."

Lucy and Rosie both pricked up their ears. That was John, who ran the animal shelter and looked after them all. And it sounded like someone had come to choose a kitten to take home with them! A new owner was what most of the animals in the shelter were waiting for, and Lucy and Rosie both rushed to the front of their pen, purring hopefully.

A little girl and her parents were walking slowly along the line of pens, peering into each one. Some of the cats and kittens took no notice. Many of them were used to being disappointed in their search for a new home.

Lucy and Rosie, in the very last pen, waited impatiently for the visitors to reach them.

"Come and see us," they purred. "We're lovely. And we're looking for a nice new home!"

"There are so many to choose from," said the girl, her eyes wide. "I wish I could take them *all* home with me!"

Her mother laughed. "I know we've got more room in the house now that Sam's left home," she said. "But I don't think we've got enough space for *all* of them!"

"Do you see one you like, Charlie?" asked her father.

Charlie looked carefully up and down the row of pens. She'd been waiting for a kitten for so long now, she could hardly believe she was getting one at last. She'd been feeling very miserable today, until her parents had surprised her by saying that she could get a kitten.

Charlie's older sister Sam had left home that morning, and gone away to college. Charlie and Sam argued a lot of the time (especially when Charlie borrowed Sam's CDs without asking), but Charlie really hadn't wanted her sister to go.

They had all gone to take Sam to her new flat, squeezing into the car that was packed to the roof with Sam's belongings.

"See you, trouble!" Sam had said, giving Charlie a hug.

"See you," said Charlie. She didn't cry very often, but she'd had to bite her lip then.

And when they'd got home, Sam's bedroom had looked *very* empty with all her posters and books and CDs missing.

But at least Charlie was getting a kitten! She had passed the animal shelter at the end of their road every day on her way to school. And always, she wished she could have a pet of her own.

Charlie cheered up even more as she peered into the cages. That ginger kitten was very pretty, and there was a tiny white one which was curled up asleep in the sun. Charlie just didn't have a clue which one to choose as she reached the last pen.

"Hello!" purred Lucy, standing up on her back legs and poking one little paw through the wire mesh. Rosie did the same, staring up at Charlie.

"Oh, these two are cute!" Charlie said. She bent down and pushed a finger through the wire. Lucy sniffed at it, while Rosie purred like an engine.

"Mum, can we go in and see these two kittens?" Charlie asked eagerly.

Lucy and Rosie glanced at each other in delight.

Charlie's father went off to fetch John, who came back carrying a large bunch of keys. It took him a long time to find the right key for Lucy and Rosie's pen.

Lucy and Rosie stood waiting impatiently. Even the older cats had opened their eyes to see what was going on. At last, John opened the door and let Charlie in.

"They're gorgeous!" said Charlie happily, as Lucy and Rosie fell over themselves trying to scramble over her trainers. She stroked them, and the kittens purred, pushing their heads against her hands.

"This one's Lucy and that's Rosie," said John with a smile. "They've been with us ever since they were born."

"Well, Charlie?" asked her mother.

Charlie frowned. It was so difficult to choose. She stroked Rosie, then giggled as Lucy attacked the trailing laces of one her trainers. "I think I'll have this one!" And she picked Lucy up and cuddled her.

"What do you mean, you'll have *this* one?" Lucy miaowed, alarmed. "What about Rosie?"

Rosie was looking anxious now too, pawing at Charlie's leg to get her attention.

"You're coming home with us, Lucy," said Charlie happily, scratching the top of the kitten's head.

"But I can't leave Rosie behind!" Lucy mewed.

"I want to come too!" Rosie yowled.

But no one was taking any notice.

"Right, you've already had a home visit from one of our staff and Lucy's had her injections. That means you can take her away with you now," John said briskly. "We'll go and find a box for her, and sort out the paperwork."

Charlie handed Lucy over to John, and they all went out of the pen.

Miaowing pitifully, Rosie tried to follow them, but John shut the door quickly so she couldn't get out.

"Lucy!" Rosie mewed. "Lucy! Don't go without me!"

But there was nothing Lucy could do. John was holding her gently but firmly, too firmly for her to escape. All she could do was miaow miserably as she was carried away, leaving her sister staring sadly after them.

Chapter Two

"Is Lucy all right, Mum?" asked Charlie anxiously as they drew up outside the Carters' house. "She hasn't stopped making a noise since we left the animal shelter."

"She's probably a bit nervous," Mrs Carter replied with a smile.

"Don't forget, all this is very new to her."

Lucy pawed the side of the cardboard carrier. "Why won't anyone listen to me?" she yowled. It was dark inside the box, and she didn't like it at all. "I want my sister!"

"Let's get her inside," said Mr Carter, turning off the engine.

Lucy stopped yowling as she felt herself on the move again. A moment or two later the flaps on top of the box opened, and Charlie reached inside.

"Come and see your new home, Lucy," she said as she lifted the kitten out.

"What about Rosie?" Lucy mewed sadly. But Charlie didn't

understand her, of course. Instead she put the kitten gently down on the living room carpet.

Even though Lucy was still very upset about leaving Rosie behind, after a moment or two she began to look around cautiously. There were lots of new things here to sniff and scratch and explore;

things which hadn't been in the pen at the animal shelter. And there was so much space! Lucy could hardly believe how big the room was. It was *much* bigger than any of the pens at the shelter.

"Look, Lucy." Charlie began to unpack the carrier bags that her father had just brought in from the car. "We went shopping before we came to the animal shelter, and we've bought you lots of things!"

Lucy watched as Charlie emptied out a whole bagful of toys. There were little balls for chasing. Some were soft and squishy, and some had a little bell in the middle which tinkled when

the ball rolled along. There was a
fluffy mouse with a long tail
made of pink wool, and an
enormous furry spider bouncing
up and down on a piece of elastic.

"What about this, Lucy?" said
Charlie, jiggling the spider up
and down in front of the kitten.

Lucy watched politely, but she

didn't really care much about the toys. She hadn't needed any toys at the shelter, because she had had Rosie to play with . . .

Apart from the toys, there was also a very snug-looking cat basket, lined with velvet.

"This is where you're going to sleep, Lucy," said Charlie.

Lucy stared miserably up at Charlie. Until now, she had always slept with Rosie. The two kittens had curled around each other so tightly, it was difficult to tell which was which. But Rosie wasn't here to share the basket with her. Lucy was all alone.

"I wish Sam could see you, Lucy," Charlie whispered. She picked Lucy up and rubbed her chin against her kitten's soft fur. "Sam's my sister, but she doesn't live with us any more. I miss her already."

"I miss *my* sister too!" Lucy yowled.

"What's the matter, Lucy?" Charlie asked worriedly. "Oh, I know! You're probably hungry." And she took Lucy into the kitchen.

"How's she doing now?" asked Mrs Carter, who was making tea.

"She still doesn't seem very happy," Charlie said with a frown. "I thought she might be hungry." She put Lucy down, and spooned some catfood into a bowl. Lucy sniffed the air. The food smelt delicious, and she *was*

hungry. As soon as the bowl was put in front of her, she began to eat quickly.

"Good girl, Lucy," said Charlie, looking relieved. But a moment or two later Lucy stopped eating, and began miaowing again.

"Oh, Lucy," Charlie said, upset. "What's wrong?"

"I'm thinking about Rosie," Lucy mewed sadly. "She might not get much to eat without me to look after her – that Winston can be a bit of a bully sometimes!"

"Mum, what's the matter with her?" Charlie asked.

"Just give her a chance to settle in," Mrs Carter said, gently stroking the kitten's back. "Are you going to carry on calling her Lucy, or are you going to give her another name?"

"No, I like Lucy," said Charlie.

"So do I!" Lucy purred, and she rubbed her head against Charlie's ankles. She was beginning to like Charlie a lot. Charlie had understood that Lucy didn't want a different name. Now all she had to do was make her new owner understand that everything would be perfect if only Rosie could come and live with them too.

Chapter Three

"Lucy, what *is* the matter with you?" Charlie asked, shaking her head sadly. "I wish I knew."

Lucy gave a tiny miaow, and then turned back to stare out of the living room window again.

"That's what she's done all week," said Mrs Carter. "She sits and stares out of the window. And it takes her ages to climb up there." She looked ruefully at the claw marks on the sofa, where Lucy had scrambled up to reach the window. "It's almost as if she's *looking* for someone."

"I *am*," Lucy miaowed sadly. Every day she sat in the window, hoping that John would turn up at the Carters' house with Rosie. They could play with all Lucy's new toys, eat a big bowlful of delicious food and then curl up together in the big comfy basket for a snooze.

But as the days passed, Lucy had begun to realise that Rosie wasn't coming. That made her feel very lonely and miserable indeed, even though Charlie had been very kind to her and had given her everything any kitten could want. Would she ever see her sister again?

"I wish you could talk, Lucy," Charlie sighed, tickling the kitten under her chin. She'd waited for a kitten for so long, and now it seemed as if Lucy didn't even *want* to be Charlie's cat. "Then I could find out what's bothering you."

"I *can* talk!" Lucy mewed. "You just don't understand me, that's all!" She rubbed her fluffy head against Charlie's hand. Lucy liked playing with her new owner, but Charlie had to go to school, and then Lucy got very bored on her own. She was worried about Rosie too. Her sister was shy, and had always relied on Lucy to look after her. Lucy couldn't bear to think of Rosie all alone in the pen at the shelter.

"Why don't you take Lucy out into the back garden?" Charlie's mum suggested. "She's got a collar and identity tag on now, and she's got to get used to going out sometime."

Lucy pricked up her ears. *Out*? Her heart began to thump with excitement. She hadn't been allowed out of the house during the week she'd been there, but if she was let outside, then she would be able to get away and go back to the animal shelter to see Rosie!

Charlie looked doubtful. "I don't want her to get lost."

"Oh, she won't be able to get out of the garden," said Mrs Carter confidently. "The fences are high, and she's far too small to climb them. She'll be quite safe."

"That's what *you* think," Lucy said to herself, feeling very determined. She just *had* to make sure that Rosie was all right – and it looked like she was going to get a chance to do so!

Eagerly, she jumped down off the windowsill and slid down the leg of the sofa, claws extended. Mrs Carter winced.

"I think we'd better get her a scratching-post!" she said, as Lucy rushed over to the door.

Charlie followed Lucy across the room. "Hey, slow down!" she laughed as Lucy skidded across the polished floor of the hall towards the back door.

Lucy scratched at the bottom

of the door, miaowing loudly.

Charlie's face lit up. "You seem a lot happier, Lucy!" she said, looking relieved. "Now don't be scared of going outside," she went on as she unlocked the door. "I'll look after you—"

Charlie didn't get the chance to say any more. As soon as the door opened just a crack, Lucy squeezed through it and rushed outside. Then she stopped on the patio and looked around eagerly, sniffing the air. But what she saw made her heart sink.

The Carters' back garden was surrounded on all sides by very high fences. There didn't seem to be any way out at all, not even a small hole that a kitten could squeeze through. Lucy looked around desperately. If she could only find a way out, she just knew that she'd be able to find her way back to the animal shelter. After all, it was only just up the road.

"Wait for me, Lucy!" Charlie laughed as the kitten suddenly raced off down the lawn.

Lucy didn't stop. She had finally spotted a way of getting out of the garden. It wasn't easy, and it would take all her strength and determination, but she was going to do it!

There were trees all round the edges of the lawn. Most of them were very tall, much too tall for Lucy to climb. She couldn't even have made it onto the very lowest branches. But there was a plant growing in the flower border, and it had grown so much that it had trailed right over the fence and down into the street that ran alongside the garden. Lucy saw that she could get right over the fence, using the thick stems of the climbing plant like a ladder.

Lucy headed straight towards the creeper. She scrambled up the main stem, clinging on with all her might.

"Lucy! What are you doing?" Charlie called, alarmed.

Lucy clung on as hard as she could, beginning to climb higher. It was very scary because although the stems were quite thick, they were also quite floppy. They bent under her weight, even though she was very light. But she kept going.

"Lucy!" Charlie raced over to her, but Lucy was just out of her reach. "Come down!"

Lucy hauled herself up onto the top of the fence. She was panting and shaking, and she had bits of leaves and twigs stuck in her coat, but she'd made it!

She looked over the fence, and was relieved to see that the plant reached almost down to the pavement on the other side.

"Keep still, Lucy!" Charlie called urgently. "I'm going to get Mum!"

Lucy looked down at her owner.

She didn't want to upset Charlie when she'd been so kind to her, but she just had to go and see Rosie! With a little mew of farewell, she disappeared over the fence.

Chapter Four

She'd done it! Lucy dropped down onto the street on the other side of the garden. She knew she had no time to waste. Charlie and Mrs Carter would soon be hot on her trail!

Lucy ran off, and then hid behind a postbox to get her

bearings. She sniffed the air intently, her whiskers twitching as she decided which way to go. Yes, she was sure she could make it to the shelter quite easily. She couldn't wait to see Rosie's face!

Lucy trotted down the street, keeping well away from the traffic. There was so much that was strange and new all around her, but Lucy kept her head down and kept going. She had only one thought in her mind – to make it safely back to Rosie.

"Oh, look, Emma," said a voice above Lucy's head all of a sudden. "Look at that sweet little kitten!"

"Isn't it cute, Natalie!" said another voice.

Lucy glanced up. Two girls were

blocking the pavement in front of her, and she couldn't really get past them. So she waited while they stroked her, and tickled her under the chin.

"I wish I had a cat," said Emma, who was blonde, and wore big-heeled shoes. "He's gorgeous."

He! Lucy thought indignantly, wishing she could be on her way.

"Yeah, he is," agreed Natalie, who was dark-haired and wore baggy tracksuit bottoms. "But isn't he a bit young to be out on his own?"

"You're right," Emma agreed. "We'd better take him back to his owner."

Time for me to go! Lucy thought. She darted forward quickly, right

through Emma's legs, and
streaked off up the road. Both
girls made a grab for her, but
missed.

That was close! Lucy thought, as
she hurried off down the street.

"Hello, Puss," said a milkman
as he came out of one of the
gardens. He put the empty bottles

he was holding on the milk float, and came towards Lucy. "Aren't you a bit young to be out on your own?"

"No, I'm not!" Lucy mewed, and dashed off. She didn't want any more kind people trying to catch her!

A few houses later, she stopped and looked back to check that the milkman wasn't following her – and it was then that she got a real shock.

"Mum! Look what I've found!" said an excited voice, and a pair of hands clamped down on Lucy and picked her up. Lucy struggled frantically and yowled, but she couldn't get away.

"Look, Mum," said the little

boy, who was carrying Lucy. He took her over to his mother, who was weeding their front garden. "I found it outside our gate."

"Oh, what a sweet little kitten!" said his mother, stroking Lucy's head. "But she's very young to be out on her own."

"Maybe she's lost," the boy suggested.

"I'm not lost," Lucy mewed crossly. "I know exactly where I'm going!"

"Well, she's got a collar on with a phone number," said the boy's mother, inspecting Lucy's ID tag. "We'd better ring her owners – they'll be worried."

Lucy struggled helplessly as the boy carried her into the house.

"Let me go!" she wailed. "I'm going to see my sister!"

"The poor little thing must be scared out of its wits," said the boy's mum as they went into the kitchen. "Listen to the noise she's making!"

Lucy gave up. Why couldn't humans understand *anything*?

"We'd better put her somewhere safe, Luke, while I ring the owner," the boy's mum went on. "Go and fetch the cardboard carrier we took Gilbert to the vet in."

"But Gilbert's only a guinea pig," Luke objected. "The box won't be big enough."

"It'll be big enough for a small kitten like that," said his mum.

"No! I don't want to go in there!" Lucy squealed as she was gently lifted into the cardboard carrier. She didn't know what a guinea pig was, but the box smelled very funny indeed.

"It won't be for long," Luke said, patting Lucy on the head before closing the flaps.

Meanwhile, his mum was dialling the Carters' number.

Lucy was in darkness. Well, almost. There was a small hole in one of the corners which was letting a tiny amount of daylight in. Eagerly, Lucy went to investigate. Whatever a guinea pig was, it must have very sharp teeth because Gilbert had begun to chew his way through the

corner of the box. Now all Lucy
had to do was make the hole a
little bit bigger . . .

Lucy began to scratch and
scrape at the hole with her sharp
little claws. The cardboard began
to tear, and the hole grew larger.
And larger. Now Lucy could poke
her head right through it.

"No answer," said Luke's mum,

replacing the receiver. "Maybe they're out looking for her – OH!"

At that very moment Lucy wriggled out of the hole in the box, and dashed for the open door.

"Come back!" Luke shouted.

Not likely! Lucy thought as she rushed off down the path.

Lucy ran as fast as she could,

until she was sure that Luke and his mum weren't following her. From then on she was careful to scurry out of sight when any humans came along – she really was fed up with kind people trying to help her!

It was a long way to the animal shelter, longer than Lucy had thought it would be. But at last, she turned the corner and saw a big sign with red and blue letters. Lucy couldn't read, but she could recognise the pictures of the cat and dog on the sign. They were the same as the ones on the shirts that the people at the animal shelter wore.

"I made it," Lucy miaowed happily. "Rosie! Rosie! I'm back!"

Chapter Five

Lucy dashed up to the gates of the shelter. They were always kept locked so that none of the animals could escape and get lost. But that didn't stop Lucy. There was a very small gap at the bottom of the gate, but it was just about big enough for Lucy to squeeze under. Then she scampered happily off towards the cat pens.

"Rosie! Rosie!" she yowled.

Rosie was curled up in a corner of her pen, feeling miserable. She had missed Lucy very much since her sister had found a new home. She hated having no one to play with, and no one to snuggle up to when she went to sleep.

Then, all of a sudden, as if by magic, she heard Lucy's voice and smelled Lucy's smell. For a moment Rosie thought she was dreaming. She rushed to the front of the pen, and saw Lucy racing towards her, tail waving madly.

"Lucy!" Rosie gasped. "It's you! It's really you!"

"Of course it's me," Lucy mewed. She tried to nuzzle Rosie through the wire mesh, licking her sister's nose with her pink tongue. "I've come back!"

By now all the other cats in all the pens, including Ginger, Tammy and Winston, had also come to see what was going on.

"What are *you* doing here?" Winston asked Lucy. "You've got a new home!"

"But I wanted to come back!" Lucy explained.

The other cats were amazed, and began to mutter and miaow to each other. They'd never heard of any cat *wanting* to come back to the shelter when they had a new home to go to!

"What *is* all this noise?" John came out of the office, and looked along the row of cat pens. "Goodness me!" he gasped as he spotted a kitten on the wrong side of the wire mesh. "Is that *Lucy*?"

"Yes, it is!" Lucy mewed.

"What on earth are you doing

here?" John asked. He frowned as he scooped Lucy up, and looked at her closely. "I'd better go and ring the Carters at once."

He pulled out his keys, and put Lucy back into her old pen with Rosie and the other cats. Then he hurried back to the office.

"I can't believe you came back," Rosie said joyfully, as she and Lucy rubbed their heads together affectionately. "Didn't you like your new home?"

"Yes, I did . . ." Lucy mewed. But although she was thrilled to see Rosie again, Lucy was now starting to feel rather worried. She had grown to love Charlie over the last week, and she liked her new home. She didn't want to live at the animal shelter again. What she *really* wanted was for Rosie to come and live at the Carters' house too. But how could she make Charlie understand that?

Lucy began to feel even more worried when, a little while later, she saw Charlie and her parents coming towards the pen with John. She and Rosie were curled up in their bed together, giving each other a wash, but as soon as Lucy spotted them, she scrambled to her feet and began to mew worriedly. She could see that Charlie was carrying a new cat basket. They'd come to collect her.

"Oh, Lucy," said Charlie sadly,

as John unlocked the pen. "Why did you come back here? Didn't you like living with us?"

Lucy felt very bad indeed when she saw how unhappy Charlie looked. "I didn't mean to upset you," she miaowed quietly, "I just wanted to see my sister, that's all."

The Carters and John came into the pen. "Come on, Lucy, time to go – again!" said John, bending down to pick her up.

"No, wait," said Charlie, stroking Lucy's head. "I don't want to take Lucy away, if she doesn't *want* to live with us."

"But I *do* want to live with you!" Lucy said loudly, "I just want Rosie to come too!" And she dashed over to Rosie, then looked up at Charlie and her parents with pleading eyes.

"Is that other kitten Lucy's friend?" Charlie asked, pointing at Rosie. "Lucy seems to like her a lot."

"Oh, she's Lucy's sister," John explained. "They've been together since they were born."

Charlie's face lit up.

"Oh!" she exclaimed. "Mum, Dad, now I know why Lucy's been so lonely – she's been missing her sister!"

Chapter Six

When Lucy heard Charlie say that, she gave a great miaow and rushed over to her. It had taken a while, but people *did* sometimes understand after all!

"Oh, Charlie," laughed Mrs Carter, "Lucy and Rosie are just kittens!"

"No, Lucy's lonely because she misses her sister!" Charlie insisted. "Just – just like I miss Sam," she added in a wobbly voice.

Lucy pawed urgently at Charlie's leg, and Rosie did the same. Charlie bent down and picked both of the kittens up.

"They certainly are pretty close," John added. "They've never been separated before."

"See?" Charlie turned to look pleadingly at her parents. "Mum, Dad, do you think . . . ?"

Lucy and Rosie both stared at Mr and Mrs Carter with wide anxious eyes.

Charlie's parents glanced at each other. "We weren't exactly expecting *two* kittens," said Mrs Carter.

"Rosie won't be any trouble," Charlie said quickly. "I'll look after both of them."

"And it's always best to have two kittens if you possibly can," John added. "Then they can amuse each other."

"That's true," said Mrs Carter thoughtfully.

"I don't suppose two kittens will be much more trouble than one," Mr Carter said with a smile.

"YES!" Charlie yelled, and hugged Lucy and Rosie close to her.

"YES!" miaowed Lucy and Rosie together.

So, for the second time, Lucy was taken away from the animal shelter to her new home, but this time Rosie went with her. This time Lucy wasn't lonely and miserable, instead she was tucked up snugly in the same basket as Rosie.

When the car pulled up outside the Carters' house, there was another surprise. The door opened, and Sam came out.

"Sam!" Charlie yelled delightedly as she climbed out of the car, holding the cat basket carefully. "What are you doing here? Look at our kittens!"

"Oh, they're gorgeous!" Sam cried. She took the basket from Charlie so she could get a good look at Lucy and Rosie.

"You didn't say you were coming home this weekend, Sam," said Mrs Carter.

Sam turned pink. "Well, I kind of missed everyone . . ." she confessed.

"Let's go in, and play with the kittens," Charlie said, trying to take the basket from Sam.

"No, I'll carry them inside," Sam insisted, hanging on to the basket.

"No, I will!" Charlie argued.

Their parents laughed. "Why can't you two get on, like Lucy and Rosie do?" Mrs Carter asked.

"OK, we'll both carry it!" Sam grinned, and she and Charlie took the basket into the house together.

"This is our new home," Lucy announced, nipping Rosie's ear affectionately.

"Don't do that!" Rosie laughed, and next second the two kittens were rolling around in their basket, pretending to fight.

Having a sister is the best thing in the whole world! Lucy thought happily. And she was glad that Charlie thought so too!